S0-ATE-579

WITHDRAWN

WITHDRAWN

PROPERTY OF INDEPENDENCE ACADEMY

THE PIG
WHO

SAVED
THE DAY

Written by Thomas Crawford   Illustrated by Judith Fringuello

Troll Associates

Copyright © 1972 by Troll Associates
All rights reserved. No part of this book may be used or reproduced
in any manner whatsoever without written permission from the publisher.
Printed in the United States of America. Troll Associates, Mahwah, N.J.

The Pig Who Saved the Day

It was a bright, sunny summer morning when Herman first came to the farm. Herman was a pig. The only pig on the farm.

A few days before, Farmer Miller and his wife had decided that they needed a pig to make their farm complete. They already had cows, sheep, goats, chickens, horses and other animals, but they did not have a pig.

So, one fine day, Farmer Miller got in his wagon and drove to market. There were many pigs for sale at the market. Farmer Miller looked at them closely. He looked at their teeth, and their eyes. He looked at their pink skins. And he looked at their little curly tails.

Some pigs were too big. Others were too small. Some were too fat and some were too thin.

But finally, one pig caught the farmer's eye. He looked just right, so the farmer bought him.

When he got back to the farm, the farmer called his wife to come out of the house and look at the new pig. Out came Mrs. Miller. She thought it was a fine pig, indeed. "What shall we name him?" asked the farmer.

"I think Herman is a nice name for a pig," said Mrs. Miller. "Let's name him Herman." Farmer Miller agreed that was a fine name, and so they named the pig Herman. All in all, they were very happy with the new addition to their farm.

But the other animals were not happy
at all. They grumbled and groaned.

"Good grief!" said the sheep, who
were very proud of their snowy white
coats. "A pig is so dirty. He'll never
have a beautiful coat like ours."

"That's certainly true enough," said the horses. "And besides, a pig is so slow. Why, he'll never be able to run as fast as we can. Really. What good is a pig, anyway?"

Then an old goat spoke up. "Why, he can't even butt with his head, the way I can," said the goat. "Look, he doesn't have any horns. And look at that silly curled tail. What a foolish looking animal." With that, the goat began laughing in a loud, braying voice.

Next it was the cow's turn to voice her objection. "I, for one, never heard of a pig who could give milk the way I can," she mooed. "Pigs' milk — Hummphh!"

And so it went, down the line of all the other animals on the farm. Each one had something bad to say about the poor pig. Of course, they all made their remarks in loud voices — so the pig would be sure to hear them. They thought if they made the pig feel as bad as possible, he might go away.

And it was true, the pig did hear them. And he did feel bad. He felt terrible! He'd never had anyone call him names before. He had been raised on a farm with lots of other pigs. And they all liked each other just fine. But here — everyone seemed to hate him. And they had never even met him! The poor pig was so unhappy, he wanted to die. And that night, if you listened very carefully, you could hear the pig sobbing his heart out in his little stall.

That didn't bother the other animals,
though. They just wanted to be rid of
that pig. They thought it disgraceful
because he liked to wallow in the mud.
After all, it was so dirty. And the way
he gulped his food down! It was down-
right piggish!

At first, the little pig thought maybe he could win the other animals over by being as friendly as he could. So, every morning, he would say "Good morning," to the cow, or the sheep or the goat — or whatever animal he first met. But the response was always the same: "Go away," they said. "We don't want a pig in this farmyard. This is a nice place and you're just going to make a mess of it."

GOOD MORNING

After a few days of this sort of treatment, the little pig gave up trying to be friends. After all, it's hard trying to be friends when no one will have anything to do with you.

But although the little pig was heart-
broken, he tried not to show it. After
all, he had some pride, too. But he was
very sad, all the same. He didn't know
what to do. He didn't want to stay
where he wasn't wanted, but where
could he go?

The next day, things got even worse. The other animals decided they were going to get rid of the pig. That meant they had to get the farmer to get rid of the pig.

So, when the farmer's wife went to the henhouse to get the eggs, the chickens hadn't laid any. Every nest was empty. The chickens simply refused to lay any more eggs until the pig was gone.

When Farmer Miller went to milk the cows, he found that the cows would not give milk. When he tried to milk them, the cows kicked the milk pail over and walked away. The cows would not give milk until the pig was gone.

The other animals were just as stub-
born. The rooster refused to crow at
dawn.

The horse would not let the farmer
put a saddle on him.

And the sheep refused to part with
their wool.

The poor farmer didn't know what to do. If things continued this way, his farm would be ruined. He told Mrs. Miller about it, too.

"It's the pig, Martha," he said. "The other animals don't like the pig. But what can we do? We need a pig on this farm."

"I'm sure I don't know the answer, Farmer Miller," said his wife. "He seems like a nice little pig to me."

All that day, Farmer Miller and his wife wondered what to do about the pig. They wondered and wondered and wondered. Finally, Farmer Miller decided what to do.

"If we keep the pig, the farm will be ruined," he said. "The other animals won't do what they're supposed to while the pig is here. There is only one thing to do.

"Tomorrow, I will kill the pig and we will have a nice ham for Sunday dinner."

With that, Mrs. Miller burst into
tears. "Oh, the poor little pig," she
cried. "He's such a nice little fellow.
And now we're going to eat him for
Sunday dinner! Boo hoo, Boo hoo,"
she sobbed.

But Farmer Miller had made his de-
cision and he would not change his
mind. The next day would be the little
pig's last.

That night, everything was quiet in the barnyard. A full moon shone in the cloudless sky, bathing the little farm in a warm yellow light. In the barn, the animals were fast asleep, including the pig, who little realized that this was his last night on the farm.

In the house, the farmer slept sound-
ly, although Mrs. Miller was a little
restless. She was thinking about the
little pig.

It was past midnight, when the little pig was awakened by a strange noise. He lifted his head and listened carefully. He heard the noise again. Something was trying to get in the barn!

Slowly, the barn door opened. It was
all the little pig could do to keep from
crying out in terror. For there, in the
moonlight, stood a big, gray wolf. His
eyes glowed like yellow coals and his
long white teeth gleamed in the moonlight. He looked very hungry.

"Well. This looks like a feast fit for a king," the wolf said loudly. He looked at the sleeping animals and hungrily licked his lips. "Yes, indeed, I have a fine appetite tonight. It will take a big meal to satisfy it."

The sound of the wolf's voice awakened the other animals. One by one, they stirred sleepily. When they saw the wolf, their eyes opened wide with fear. They were so frightened, they couldn't make a sound.

"Listen to me," hissed the wolf. "The first one who makes a sound is the first one I will eat. I am very hungry to-night and I don't want that farmer disturbing my meal."

Then the wolf began walking slowly around the barn. He looked at the sheep — especially the fat and tender little lambs. He looked at the cows — especially the delicious little calves. And the goats. And the horses. And all the animals in the barn. All the animals looked so tasty the wolf could not make up his mind. Finally, he stopped in front of the sheep. He had made up his mind. "I am going to eat this tender and juicy little lamb," he announced as all the animals squeezed toward the back of their stalls. Suddenly, a high little voice said, "STOP!"

"Who said that?" growled the wolf.

"I did," said the voice. It came from the pig's stall. The wolf went over.

"I was going to eat that little lamb," he growled, "but since you made the first sound, I'm going to eat you instead."

"You'll have to catch me first," cried
the little pig.

With that, he leaped out of the stall,
past the startled wolf, and right out
the barn door. With a snarl of rage,
the wolf ran after the fleeing pig.

Around and around the barnyard
they went, the pig running for his life,
and the big wolf hot on his heels.

The other animals crowded at the
door of the barn, watching the furious
chase. Try as he would, the wolf could
not catch the little pig. In fact, if you
have ever tried to catch a pig yourself,
you know it is very difficult.

Back and forth, they went in the moonlight, with the wolf getting angrier and angrier because he could not catch the swift little pig. By now, the pig was squealing loudly, because he hoped the farmer would hear the noise and wake up. He knew he could not run much longer and then the wolf would be on him.

Suddenly, the lights went on in the farmhouse. A few moments later, the farmer stuck his head out the window. "What's going on out here?" he cried.

Then he saw the little pig leading the wolf a merry chase around the barnyard. Quick as a flash, the farmer got his gun, and dashed out of the house. He took careful aim in the moonlight and pulled the trigger.

BLAM! The wolf fell dead. Just in time, too, for the little pig could not have held out another minute.

Of course, after that, the pig was a
hero. All the animals on the farm realized they owed their lives to the pig.
Suddenly, they knew how badly they
had treated him. One by one, the animals went to the pig and apologized
for the mean things they had said.

This made the pig very happy. He wanted nothing more than to live in peace with the other animals on the farm. And that is just what happened. No one ever insulted the pig again.

Farmer Miller and his wife treated the pig very well. Not only didn't they have him for dinner, but he got the best corn and grain to eat and the farmer built him a beautiful new stall.

This was only fitting. For after all,
he was the pig who saved the day.